Richard Scarry's
Sniff
the Detective

A Golden Book • New York
Western Publishing Company, Inc., Racine, Wisconsin 53404

Western Publishing offers a wide range of fine juvenile and adult activities, games, and puzzles. For more information write Golden Press, 120 Brighton Road, Dept. M, Clifton, NJ 07012.

Sniff Catches the Robber

Sniff is a detective.

He helps people find things.

He helps catch bad people.

He thinks with his head.

And he smells with his nose.

One day Sniff got a phone call.
It was Chief Hound.
"We need your help," Hound said.
"Meet me at Mrs. Jewel's house."
"I will be there right away,"
said Sniff.

"How can I help?" Sniff asked.
Hound said, "This is Mrs. Jewel.
And this is her bracelet box.
Mrs. Jewel likes to wear
a lot of bracelets.
She likes it even better than
eating pumpkins. She grows
pumpkins in her garden.

"Every morning Mrs. Jewel opens
her bracelet box. She takes
out some bracelets to wear.
Every morning she sees
that another bracelet is missing."

"I have lost seven bracelets,"
said Mrs. Jewel.
"This must stop!
Soon I will have no bracelets left."

"Have you gone out this week?"
asked Sniff.
"Yes," said Mrs. Jewel, "but only
to water my pumpkins."

"Has anyone been here?"
asked Sniff.
"No," said Mrs. Jewel.
"Have you left a window open?"
"No," said Mrs. Jewel, "and I always
lock the back door."

Sniff thought and thought.
At last he said,
"I will help you.
I will stay here.
I will be quiet.
I will watch. I will listen."

The sun went down.
Mrs. Jewel went to sleep.
She made lots of noise.
She snored and snored.

Sniff listened.
He heard something.
He thought he smelled a rat.
Raffles Rat was in the room!

Raffles quickly went to
Mrs. Jewel's bracelet box.
He opened it.
He took out a bracelet.
Raffles climbed up the chimney.
Sniff could not catch him.

Raffles Rat had escaped
up the chimney.
"If he comes back again,
I know how to catch him,"
said Sniff to himself.
"I have just the right kind
of bracelet for him."

The next night Sniff watched again.
But he soon fell asleep.
Raffles Rat came down the chimney.
He saw a small bracelet
that opened and closed.
It was the right size for his wrist.
He snapped it shut on his wrist.

Raffles Rat then climbed quickly
up the chimney.
Oh, look! Sniff has been dragged
out of his chair.
Sniff had tied the small bracelet
to his leg with a string.
The bracelet was a handcuff!
Raffles could not get the bracelet
off his wrist and escape.

Mrs. Jewel pulled Raffles
out of the chimney.
Chief Hound came into the room.
"Where did you hide
the bracelets, Raffles?"
asked Chief Hound.
Raffles told him.

Chief Hound found eight bracelets
in a pumpkin in the garden.
"We must celebrate," said Mrs. Jewel.
So they all sat down and had
pumpkin pie.
Then Chief Hound took Raffles
off to jail.
Raffles will never steal
another bracelet again,
especially not one with
a string on it!

Sniff's Best Case Ever

One day Sniff woke up.
It was raining.
"I am tired," he thought.
"I am glad I have
nothing to do."

Just then Sniff got a phone call.
It was the police chief
in another city.
"We need your help!" he said.
"I will come right away,"
said Sniff.

Sniff was not happy.
He did not want to go.
The next day was his birthday.
He wanted to stay home.
He wanted to eat cake and ice cream.
But Sniff had work to do!

Sniff had to take the train.
He had to ride all night.
Hurry, Sniff!
Don't miss the train!

SLEEPING-CAR

"Look at all these
scary guys!" Sniff thought.
"Who are they?

"They are wearing sunglasses.
They are looking at me!"

Sniff went to his bedroom
on the train.
He hid under the bed.

More scary guys got on the train.
They all carried violins.
Sniff was afraid.
What were they up to?

At last it was morning.
Sniff came out from
under the bed.
He saw all the scary guys.
They were looking at him.

The sun was shining.
So Sniff put on sunglasses, too.
He stepped outside.

But the scary guys threw away
their sunglasses.
Then Sniff saw who they were.
They were all police chiefs.
They had come from many cities.

They were playing violins.
They were singing,
"Happy birthday to you,
dear Sniffy."
It was a surprise party!

So they all went to the beach.
They played ball.
They went for a swim.
They ate cake and ice cream
until they could eat no more.

And Sniff had the best
birthday ever!